The Dream Trials

Painted Wings Publishing

The Story Behind The Story

A fellow author, Monroe Wildrose, put out a call to compile a fairy tale retellings anthology featuring midsize to plus-size young adult female protagonists. My first attempt at creating a short story for submission was a bit of a failure because I strayed pretty far from the source material. I still love it, but it's more of an 'inspired by' story than a true retelling. (It can be read in ebook or paperback: *The Hatanii Bride.*)

This is my second go at a fairy tale retelling. I wanted something less common than the well-known Disney ones. Ironically, I decided to transform *The Princess & the Pea* as I lay unable to sleep one night. The Danish tale is surprisingly simplistic, which gave me room to expand on it. I latched on to the prince needing a wife, the rainfall, the twenty mattresses and the pain, and so much more, wrapping it up in dreamer magic and romance.

A shorter version of this retelling can be found in *Femme Fairytales*, an anthology with several other authors and their tales that fit the theme. I highly recommend grabbing it and enjoying them all!

I decided to publish this version separately with extra custom touches, including an entire bonus scene of Jonas's coronation day. The original submission wasn't able to include that scene due to a word count limitation.

If you're looking for even more, **Jonas's bonus scenes** are a real treat, and can be downloaded by newsletter subscribers! To access them and more, go to JHouserWrites.com

Book-related merch can also be purchased on my author website!

The Dream Trials

J. HOUSER

Painted Wings Publishing

Chapter One

Maribel stood in the hatter's shop, sorting through the available ribbons with her best friend, Celia. Maribel loved fashion, reading, long walks, and learning new things. She and Celia had planned for some time to update their accessories, and the hatter carried an astounding selection.

"I rather like this one," Maribel said, draping a deep plum ribbon over her hand. It complemented her skin tone well.

Celia glanced at the ribbon, shrugging. "I think the buttercup yellow is more fetching."

They may be best friends, but they were night and day. Celia was a tall, thin redhead, covered in freckles. Maribel's complexion was darker, and she had always been shorter and heavier than Celia. They rarely agreed on fashion, but they'd grown up together, and shared other interests.

Maribel set the ribbon in her wicker shopping basket to consider. She'd never been a fan of yellow; Celia could choose it for herself if she so desired.

Humming, Maribel ran her finger along the edge of the cut ribbon bin. The precut odds and ends were cheaper, and her mother had reminded her to keep to a strict budget. Smiling, Maribel snatched up a pretty pea green one with generous length. It had scalloped edges. "Ooh, I like this."

Celia plucked a brand-new spool of bright pink ribbon from a nearby shelf. "Green again? Why not something brighter like this?"

"What's wrong with green?" It had always been Maribel's favorite color. Celia joked that it had to be because the prince's eyes were green, but in all her eighteen years, Maribel had never even met the man. He *did* have green eyes, but her favorite color hadn't been determined by the physical attribute of a man she'd yet to meet.

"Variety," Celia simply stated, depositing the pink spool into her own basket.

Maribel was undeterred. Fretting over someone else's idea of fashion dos and don'ts seemed like a pretty foolish way to spend one's time. She gathered the loose ribbon and put it with the purple one.

"Clouds are rolling in," the hatter's assistant said, staring out the shop windows into the open market.

A gong rang in the distance, and they all paused.

It can't be. The gong resided at the castle, and was only used for special warnings and celebrations.

A heartbeat later, the gong rang again. Maribel and Celia shared a hesitant look. *Please don't let there be a third…* There were no planned celebrations in the kingdom that day, but the people had been put on alert…

A third time, the gong rang through the air, then fell silent.

Maribel swallowed.

"She's gone," the hatter's assistant whispered.

"She's gone," Maribel echoed, her chest tight.

Official word had been delivered across the kingdom some weeks ago, warning the citizens to be prepared for the death of the queen. She had been a kind and wise queen. In fact, Maribel had never heard a single person utter anything truly negative about the woman.

Solemnly, Celia set her basket down. "Come on, then."

Maribel perched her basket on the ribbon bin, joining her. The hatter emerged from the back workroom, and followed the girls outside with his assistant. The entire open-air market was lined with citizens now. People filed out of shops and the church at the end of the town square.

It was tradition to pay their respects at the passing of royalty. When the gong rang again, everyone bowed their heads, silent for a full minute.

As the minute began, a rain droplet fell onto Maribel's neck, to the side of her braid. There hadn't even been clouds in the sky a half hour ago. She dutifully kept her head bowed, tears pricking at her eyes as she focused on the loss of their beloved queen.

Another drop moistened Maribel's arm. And a couple more landed in unison on her back.

The gong rang a final time, and everyone stood straight.

The rain picked up quickly, and most people retreated inside.

Maribel and Celia didn't, however. At least a dozen other maidens remained in the open market, also oddly entranced by the rainfall.

Even as the heavens pelted them, they smiled. The rain was warm, iridescent, and otherworldly. There was something almost magical about it. It was like a hug from the beloved queen herself, as a goodbye to her people.

Maribel wasn't accustomed to standing in the open during showers, but it was a beautiful moment she wanted to drink in. She lifted her face to the sky, allowing the rain to spatter her skin, to soak into her hair and clothing, to drain down her neck and legs.

The storm was brief, but Maribel was grateful for the cleansing moment nature had given them during a time of mourning.

Celia giggled, wiping drenched hair out of her eyes. "We should finish our shopping." She hooked her arm through Maribel's, and they reentered the shop.

The hatter had returned to his work in the back. His assistant eyed the girls as they entered. "Why would you choose to get soaked to the bone like that?"

Maribel couldn't stop smiling, despite having been on the brink of tears minutes earlier. "It was wonderful. Couldn't you feel it?"

The assistant rolled their eyes, pointing to the window. "It was something only young maidens were foolish enough to do. Have your parents not taught you better?"

Pursing her lips, Maribel shot Celia a look. Neither of their parents would be pleased to have them waltz into their homes drenched.

"It was special rain," Celia said, defiantly squaring her shoulders.

Heading back to their stool by the counter, the assistant huffed. "Then I hope your purchases make up for me having to mop the floor again today."

Maribel glanced down, guilt washing over her. They'd already dripped all over, a nice puddle forming at their feet. "Oh, I'm sorry."

She was supposed to stop by a few more shops, and hadn't planned on spending her entire allowance at the hatter's, but she generously loaded up her basket and paid for much more ribbon than she needed, emptying her coin pouch to make up for the hassle.

Soggy, the girls strolled toward their homes with their goods, marveling over the rain. "Have you ever felt something like that?" Celia asked.

"No, but it was lovely," Maribel replied.

Celia sidestepped a puddle. "And now we wait to hear more about the prince taking the throne." She grinned. "And taking a bride."

Maribel couldn't help but wrinkle her nose. It felt too early to talk about that. The king and queen had only been able to bear one child—a son—later in life. The king had died two years ago, and the prince was their only heir. The law required him to take the throne within thirty days of his mother's death, and to pick a bride to rule alongside him. Tradition dictated he choose a commoner in the kingdom.

"There are a lot of eligible girls," Maribel said. "And I can't imagine he's excited to start sorting through them all while he's grieving…"

A passing mother nodded at them, and her young boy hopped into a large puddle. The mother gasped. "Daniel!"

Maribel and Celia stifled laughs as the little boy apologized.

"You're not even dreaming *at all* of living in the castle?" Celia asked, wringing her hair again.

They were both of an age to marry, and the prince was only a year older, but the chance of either of them being picked was slim to none. "The castle is probably drafty," Maribel kidded. "And what if he chooses his queen based on stupid criteria? Like which maiden can swim the fastest?"

Celia laughed. "Swimming?"

"Yes. In a lake full of swamp beasts." She grinned wickedly, and Celia laughed again.

"What if it's about favorite colors? What if he *hates* green because he hates his own eyes?" Celia asked comically. "It would be quite the scandal."

Maribel feigned amazement. "What if he chooses based on what he *sees* with his eyes?" She pinched Celia's thin arm. "Maybe he doesn't like scrawny girls…" She poked her own gut. "Or thick ones. Because if that's the case, neither of us will be chosen."

Her own eyes wide, Celia nodded. "Maybe I should start visiting the church more often to find a way to gain his favor… An answer to a prayer…"

Drawing herself back from their moment of levity, Maribel sighed. She had time to plan out her life, and it was futile to chase the unknown desires of a man in power whom she may never even meet. And…

"Let's be respectful." She straightened her posture. "I'm sure he's taking things one day at a time. He's probably not even worried about that until after the funeral." Maribel raised an eyebrow in censure. "And Her Majesty deserves the respect of full mourning."

Celia cocked her head to the side. "True. She'll be missed."

"Yes. No more talk about the prince and some random girl out there…"

After they arrived at their lane and parted ways, Maribel walked into her home and set down her bulging satchel of ribbons.

"Did you fall in the stream on your way back?" Maribel's mother fussed over her on her return.

"I'm fine. It was just the rain."

Her mother frowned, caressing her cheek. "We'll all miss her."

Maribel nodded. The kingdom had lost a treasure today.

"But why in the world did you stay out in the rain? It was only sprinkling during the short observance."

Maribel couldn't resist smiling again. "It was beautiful."

Her mother raised her eyebrows high. "It was only rain. Go change before you catch a cold!"

Maribel did as told. Her mother fussed far too much. She was already eighteen; she didn't need to be told how to take care of herself. As she stripped her clothes in her room, she mused over the rain, though. *Only* rain? It had been beautiful, like nothing Maribel had ever experienced.

When Maribel emerged from her room, her mother stood at the stove stirring split pea soup for their supper. She forced Maribel to sit at the kitchen table and guzzle piping hot bone broth as a precaution to ward off illness. Maribel's younger sister and brother played in the backyard, only joining her and their mother when their father returned from work.

As she retired to bed early that evening, Maribel could have sworn another storm was brewing outside, as the soft pitter-patter of rain lulled her to sleep.

Chapter Two

"I love the smell of the earth after fresh rain. Don't you?" Celia commented as they chatted in Maribel's sitting room, sorting through their stash of old and new ribbons.

"You too?" Maribel's mother asked, poking her head in. "Maybe I'm the mad one here…" She proceeded to stroll past the open door.

Celia looked to Maribel, confused.

"I said the same thing this morning, but she swears it didn't rain last night…" And it *was* odd, because there had been no mud, no signs of rain come morning, but Maribel had heard it herself as she'd fallen asleep, and that fresh dewy smell had enlivened her as she rose.

Maribel stacked her ribbon by color and length. Almost half her collection was green; maybe she ought to try more colors after all.

"And then I had the wildest dream…" Celia continued minutes later, massaging her shoulder. "I was crossing under a bridge, and an old beggar asked me for help with carrying something."

Stilling, Maribel listened. The dream was eerie, for she too had had a dream like that the night before.

Celia wrapped a long cream ribbon around her hand. "So, I helped the poor man, but gosh his bag was *heavy*! The strap of the bag dug into my shoulder. I know it was just a dream, but it felt so real." She rubbed her shoulder again.

Wide eyed, Maribel stared at her. That had almost exactly been her same dream. She'd woken with a sore shoulder; it still ached. "That's mad… I … had a dream like that too."

"Really?" Celia narrowed her eyes.

"Yes, but Mother said it was just my mattress." Her father's business had been doing poorly lately, and they couldn't afford to replace the lumpy mattress anytime soon.

Brushing off the bizarre coincidence, Celia smiled. "Too weird."

As Maribel went to bed that night, she felt around her mattress. It wasn't the most comfortable, but it wasn't like it was made of rocks. Luckily, the soreness in her shoulder had eased around midday, and she was ready to put the odd shared dream behind her.

After blowing out her candle, she climbed under her quilt, ready for sleep to claim her. Rain sang her to sleep for the second night.

Maribel blinked. She stood in the middle of a busy cobblestone lane. "What the…" How had she gotten there? The midday sun beat down on her, the breeze nonexistent.

She glanced around, trying to piece it together. What did she even remember last? She ought to remember walking somewhere… Though no pain remained in her shoulder, she rubbed it. *The dream.* Could this be another dream? It was so vivid, so real, but her dream the previous night had also started abruptly.

Shoes clicked on the cobblestone, and mumbles of passersby surrounded her, though no one paid her any attention.

Maribel stopped a passing man. "Sir, uh, what day is it?"

"Tuesday, miss." He gave her a single nod and continued walking.

She bit her lip. Tuesday? If her recollection was correct, she'd gone to bed Tuesday night, so this was perhaps a memory from hours before? But she'd spent the whole day with Celia, and hadn't stepped foot in this lane…

Sharp pain stung her toe. "Ah!"

A little boy had randomly stomped on her foot.

"Thadeus!" a woman scolded. She turned to Maribel. "I'm so sorry. He can be unruly sometimes. Are you okay?"

Still in a great deal of pain, Maribel lied. "I'm fine. He's just a little one."

"Thank you," the woman said, exasperated. "Is there anything I can do for you?"

Maribel clenched her teeth, tears pricking at her eyes. How had that small of a child inflicted *so much pain*? "I'm all right."

The boy's mother gave her an apologetic smile, then ran after him, stopping him from wreaking more havoc down the lane.

Blowing out a breath, Maribel stood on one leg. "I need something for my foot…" A cool stream to dip her aching toes in would do wonders.

The next thing she remembered was waking to morning sunlight pouring in through her windows.

She furrowed her brow. *Huh…* Her toe still throbbed. A lumpy mattress couldn't be blamed for a sore toe, could it? She had to have kicked the wooden bed frame during the night, and it had inspired the dream… That was all—a perfectly reasonable explanation.

After making her bed, she approached the window. No signs of rain again, but that fresh scent filled her lungs. Had she hit herself on the head at some point?

A heartbeat later, a tap on the bedroom door claimed her attention. "Are you up, dear?" her mother asked.

Maribel drew a deep breath. "Yes, I'll be right out." It was the queen's funeral service that day, and they would want to leave the house early to get a good place for the public observance. Maribel chose a forest green dress of a respectable length for the observance, tying her new pea green ribbon around her waist. The queen had loved bright colors, and had stated her people should reflect hope in their mourning.

Maribel's family joined the throngs who gathered along the path the queen's casket would travel. The queen would be laid to rest at the royal cemetery, but this gave the citizens a chance to offer their last goodbyes.

Her toe still sore, Maribel used the distraction to avoid crying too much about the queen. She'd been devastated at the king's funeral because his death hadn't been anticipated. But she'd always adored the queen, looking up to her as much as she did her own mother. She'd even met the queen once during her years in primary school.

After what must have been a full hour, the crowd to Maribel's right hushed. She stood on her tippy-toes. It was worth the pain to see past the people in front of her.

Horseshoes clapped on the stone path, the giant regal creatures pulling the queen's flower-laden casket through the street on a lovely cart. Maribel's heart hurt.

The prince's carriage kept pace behind the funeral cart. Facing forward, Prince Jonas wore a solemn look, as would be expected.

After the royal funeral procession had passed, the crowd stirred. Parents with crying children departed, as well as many adults who likely had to get back to work. Maribel's father was one of them. He kissed Maribel and her younger siblings on the head, and his wife on the cheek. "Sorry, but I don't have much choice. Someone needs to tend the shop."

Maribel was the oldest of three, and her little sister was restless.

"Follow the crowds to the services, or return home?" their mother asked.

"Services," Maribel answered, while her two siblings in unison voted for home. She couldn't blame them. Funerals could be long and taxing, and it would be a decent walk to and from the official services. "I'll be fine alone. I'd like to go."

Her mother smiled. "Okay. You be careful."

Maribel nodded, trailing the others in the street who chose to follow the funeral procession. Not far down the path, she ran into Celia with her family.

"Is it all right if I join?"

"Of course, dear," Celia's mother replied.

The group walked in near silence for some time. With each footstep, Maribel's toe ached. She leaned against Celia, whispering. "My toe hurts from last night…"

Celia immediately gave her a shocked look. "Yes… Mine too. Another dream?"

Maribel nodded. How could it happen two nights in a row? She'd never shared a dream with someone before, not that it was sharing exactly, since they hadn't seen each other in the dreams. "A little boy stomped on my foot."

It was Celia's turn to nod. "Yes, such a brat."

Shrugging, Maribel hooked her arm around Celia's. "He was just a little child."

Celia rolled her eyes. "Well, call him what you like, but I draw the line at that kind of rude behavior. I gave his mother an earful."

Maribel almost laughed. "It wasn't that bad. And it was only a dream…"

"But was it?"

It had to have been, right? And even if it hadn't been, children could learn…

"What about the rain?" Maribel asked. "I fell asleep to it again, and woke to the fresh air, but there were no signs of it in the morning."

Narrowing her eyes, Celia scratched her temple. "Come to think of it, I fell asleep to it, but I didn't notice that smell in the morning."

Maribel's mind worked. "Do you think—"

Celia's mother softly shushed them.

Embarrassed, Maribel clamped her mouth closed.

After ages of plodding alongside other townspeople, they arrived at the head church. Flowers of every color flooded the area. The clergyman gave a speech, as did esteemed government officials and beloved family members.

Prince Jonas stood last to address the crowd. It wasn't exactly an appropriate time to make the observation, but Maribel couldn't deny he was devastatingly handsome. He had a sharp jawline, neatly trimmed brown hair, and those lovely green eyes. She'd seen him before while attending less-somber public events, and at the king's funeral. He hadn't spoken at his father's funeral, so this was Maribel's first time actually hearing his voice.

He stood at the pulpit, thanking his people for attending. "My mother would be honored to know how many have taken the time to pay their respects." He was elegant, not a hair out of place as he continued his speech. His voice light and confident, he shared a couple of heartwarming stories that made Maribel tear up. He seemed on the verge of tears as well, and her heart fully went out to him. He was young to take over the kingdom, but he swore to do his best to carry on his parents' legacy.

After he sat, the clergyman said a few last words, then dismissed the people. The crowds shuffled away, including Celia's family, but Celia and Maribel clung to the edges of some bushes to wait for others to pass. They'd walk home together when it wasn't so stifling.

Maribel's eyes were glued to the prince. "He looks so sad." It was the most obvious and least eloquent thing she could have said, but it was true. He stood on the stage yards away, the image of duty as he discussed matters with those in charge of the service.

"I wish they'd explain his selection process," Celia said.

The public knew the required timeframe for him to choose a bride, and the tradition that it had to be a maiden from the kingdom, but not much else had ever been shared about how the royal family selected brides and grooms to join them on the throne. Rumor had it Prince Jonas had briefly courted a neighboring kingdom's princess, and another local maiden at some point, but he didn't seem to have anyone in his sights at the moment.

Shrugging, Maribel replied, "I don't think it really matters how he chooses, does it? As long as they're a good king and queen…"

"I guess…"

Maribel gestured in his direction. "Don't you feel sorry for him, though? He's having to lay his mother to rest, take over the kingdom, and choose to marry a stranger all in a month's time."

Celia scoffed. "No, I don't feel sorry for him. It's probably a lot to deal with, but I refuse to pity a wealthy, powerful, handsome man who gets his pick of the ladies from an entire kingdom."

Annoyed but not wanting a fight, Maribel let it go. Whomever he chose, the girl had a choice in the matter.

"Plus," Celia added, "he's probably been secretly courting someone for ages, and will just pretend he's plucked her from a local town soon."

That had to be jealousy rearing its ugly head. Celia was as interested in the prince as Maribel was, if not more. "Anyway…"

Most of the attendees had cleared out quickly, but several small children and their parents lined up to greet the prince. He bent and gave the children gracious smiles and handshakes. Maribel's heart melted. She and Celia had been so curious about him over the years. He didn't go out into crowds or give arrogant smiles as one would expect a prince to. He'd always kept to himself during public events. Was it because he was stuffy and full of himself? Maribel would like to think he was kind, and didn't consider himself so much above his people. Generosity to children was a good sign, but that could also just be a politician's move.

"Want to come to my place?" Celia asked. "Spend lunch with us?"

Maribel returned her focus to her friend. "Yes, let's do that."

Chapter Three

Maribel quadruple-checked that the skies were clear that night. The moon glowed brightly, no hints of inclement weather on the horizon. After she brushed her teeth, crawled under her quilt, and closed her eyes, rain *somehow* pattered against the window she'd just looked through. She slid a hand to pull back her quilt to go check, but before she could do so, she'd drifted to sleep.

Blinking, she found herself sitting at a study desk, staring at a man who couldn't actually be there. "Mr. Hamon?" He had been one of her teachers years ago, but had fallen ill and since passed.

He gave her a bright smile under his thick white mustache. "Who else would you expect for your test today?"

"I…" She cocked her head. "This *is* a dream, then… Right?"

He simply shrugged. "Does it matter?"

She gaped. "A little? I'm not accustomed to seeing dead people…"

Chuckling, he stacked a few papers on a desk. "No need to fear. It's a simple test."

Wary, she eyed him. "If I don't want to take it?"

"It's your choice."

"And if I fail…?"

The elderly gentleman twisted his lips. "You'll move on with your life."

But I won't move on with my life if I don't *fail?* She shook the cobwebs away in her brain. It was just a silly dream. At least she wouldn't wake with a sore toe or shoulder… "All right. What questions do you have for me?"

They had to have spent hours exchanging questions and answers. He challenged her memory on the most basic of arithmetic, and on the uppermost limits of her science courses and literacy. A good portion of time was dedicated to geography and history of the world and their kingdom. Maribel was proud of herself for how well it had gone.

She woke in the morning, breathing in the impossibly fresh aroma of rain. This time, her dream had granted her the pain of a headache. Then again, she'd probably just hit her head on a different bedpost, right? Because the idea of physical tokens of pain after strangely lucid dreams was just…

Gnawing on willow bark for the pain later that morning, she met up with Celia to go for a stroll through the nearby woods.

"Need some willow bark?" Maribel offered. "I grabbed another bit for you in case you needed it."

Celia gave her a confused look as she stepped over a large rock in their path. "What for?"

"Headache from the dream last night…"

"That doesn't sound fun. But why would *I* need willow bark for *your* headache?"

A light breeze rustled the leaves in a tree overhead. "I just assumed you had the same dream last night again."

Furrowing her brow, Celia considered. "I don't remember having a dream last night."

"Oh…"

"I honestly can't remember the last time I had a dream."

Maribel halted. "What are you talking about? What about the two prior nights?"

Celia faced her. "What about them? I don't remember any dreams."

Too stunned to speak, Maribel stared at her a moment. "But… The… What about the odd rain at night and in the morning?"

"Are you pulling a joke on me?" Celia smiled. "It hasn't rained since the passing of the queen."

Neither mischief nor guile tainted any of her words.

Maribel rubbed the back of her neck. "I…." What was she supposed to say to that?

"How about we call on Athena while we're in the area?" Celia asked innocently.

"Sure…" Maribel muttered, fully perplexed.

After walking a ways off their path, they reached the homestead of Celia's cousin, Athena. The three of them had spent countless hours together studying, exploring, and chatting.

Athena greeted them with hugs, and welcomed them in. "Tea, anyone?"

Both Maribel and Celia accepted.

"Lovely. I'll put the kettle on."

Since they'd known each other for several years, Maribel felt she could be trusted. "I'm going to help her in the kitchen," she told Celia. Celia was unbothered, still working on a knot in her hat ribbons.

"Thanks for the tea," Maribel cautiously said as she entered the kitchen.

"Of course." Athena smiled, tucking her black curls behind her ear.

Fidgeting with her hands, Maribel second-guessed herself, but she persisted. "Has Celia been acting weird around you the last couple of days?"

Athena shook her head. "Well, I haven't seen her all week. What's wrong?"

Maribel held her tongue, unsure. *She* was the one dreaming of dead and imaginary people, then remembering things wrong. Was she certain she hadn't hit her head recently?

Wincing, Athena rubbed her temple.

Maribel paused. "Headache?"

"Yes. Long night," Athena said dismissively.

Maribel eyed her. Athena was only a couple of years older than she and Celia were. "Any weird dreams lately?"

Squinting, Athena answered. "Yes…"

"A beggar, a little boy, and a—"

"Schoolteacher?"

A squeak escaped Maribel's mouth as she pointed at an equally shocked Athena.

"How would you know that?" Athena asked, all surprise.

"Me too," Maribel whispered.

"Is there a mouse in here?" Celia asked playfully from behind Maribel.

"No. We were just talking about—" Athena started.

Maribel slid a finger to her lips where Celia couldn't see.

Athena did a double take. "Talking about, uh … the prince. Who else?"

"Save some gossip for me. I'm going to freshen up."

"Will do," Maribel choked out.

Celia's footsteps padded down the hallway.

"Why did you stop me?" Athena whispered. "You said she was acting weird. Doesn't that mean she's having the dreams too?"

Maribel shook her head. "The weird thing is that she *stopped* having them after two nights. Then forgot about them completely, and about the impossible nighttime rain!"

Athena's mind worked. "Yes, the rain."

"Do you know anyone else experiencing this?"

"No. But I could ask…"

"Yes. Let's ask around. But … carefully. I don't want everyone thinking we're mad or bewitched…"

After a short and awkward visit, Maribel excused herself to walk home alone. Though her headache had subsided, she clung to that excuse. With each footstep along the path, Maribel pondered the unbelievable circumstances. Could magic be at play here? She kept thinking of the rain at the queen's passing. Perhaps it had been cursed, but to what end?

Unable to shake the eerie feeling about the shared dreams, Maribel diverted from her route to pay a couple more homes a visit. She didn't want to alarm anyone, so she'd ask cautiously generic questions about rain and dreams, but nothing specific, then gauge their responses.

She first stopped at the home of her nearest aunt and uncle. Maribel's male cousins seemed utterly disinterested in her questions, and the female cousins were simply confused.

"Has it rained since the queen's death?" Maribel asked.

Her cousins Gwyneth and Eden looked at her strangely as the three of them sat together. She wouldn't normally ask them for a weather report.

"No…" answered Eden, the older of the two. At the time of the queen's death, she and her fiancé had been visiting his family, and had ducked back inside as soon as possible after the gong had released them from the minute of silence for the queen's passing.

"I heard the rain was horrendous," Gwyneth said.

Eden turned on her. "*Heard* the rain was horrendous? You didn't observe the queen's passing?"

"I…" Gwyneth grappled for words. "I didn't hear the gongs," she shyly confessed.

"And what, pray tell, were you doing in the *middle of the day* where you could not hear the castle's gongs?" They lived close enough to hear the on-site gongs, not those used as relays across the kingdom.

The room was thick with tension as Gwyneth swallowed, staring at her hands in her lap.

"Were you with Fasol at the time?"

And *that* was Maribel's cue to excuse herself. Both cousins were older than her, so they could make their own choices, but the impropriety of the situation still punctuated the issue, and she had not come for drama. Fasol was the son of the local baker, and Maribel had noticed he and Gwyneth were rather cozy, but they hadn't announced any plans to wed…

"I just wanted to drop by for a *short* visit." Maribel jabbed a thumb over her shoulder, standing.

"Stay!" Gwyneth insisted.

No thank you. "I, uh… Mother needed me to run an errand. I forgot…"

After excusing herself, she stopped by her friend Hailey's home. Hailey had also had the dreams, and agreed to ask around more.

Chapter Four

Over the next several days, Maribel was greeted with the same cycle over and over—vivid dreams, echoes of pain, and the sounds and smells of rain caressing her sleep. A new body part ached each morning, and she lied to her mother every time she asked about Maribel limping or rubbing a sore spot. She blamed it on the old lumpy mattress. Aside from not wanting anyone to think she was mad, she also didn't want to concern anyone until she got to the bottom of it.

Hailey lasted a couple of days longer with the dreams than Celia had before she forgot it all, her memories of the strange coincidence wiped. With Hailey having forgotten everything, Maribel also lost the connection to any friends Hailey had been keeping track of who had also shared the dreams.

On the fourteenth night of dreams, Maribel drifted to sleep, 'waking' in a cave. Only a brightly burning torch lit the large chamber she stood in, foreboding filling her chest, the desire to retreat strong.

She glanced over her shoulder. The path across the chamber continued behind her.

A haunting low rumble bounced off the stone walls. A giant pair of red-orange eyes blinked from the shadows of the path in front of her. They swirled like pools of lava, nothing good in their depths. Maribel could hardly breathe.

A footfall thumped, claws scratching. And another.

Her heart raced.

With another step forward, the creature showed itself—a dragon.

"Oh no…" Maribel whispered, her voice shaky. Her palms became clammy as she eased backward.

Not a single dragon had been spotted in the kingdom in decades, not even in the northern territories. From what she'd been taught, this was a small one, but it was still three times her size, densely muscled and not easily dismissed.

It scraped another step forward, its growl low. She retreated another footstep, holding her hands up. "Nice dragon?"

Its eyes narrowed as smoke plumed from its slits of nostrils. And far behind Maribel, voices rose, full of panic.

"Come on, we need to get out of here," a woman shouted. Maribel almost agreed, until the woman spoke again. "Hurry, Thadeus, we need to run!"

"Mamma, I'm stuck," the little boy cried.

Maribel's heart froze as the dragon's gaze shifted beyond her. Perhaps it wanted something leaner, something more tender, or more of a buffet.

This is just a dream. It can't hurt you or anyone else.

The little boy cried. "Ouch, Mamma."

"Hold still while I get you loose."

It felt *completely* real.

Maribel wasn't ready to die, nor was she okay with letting innocent people outside the cave be devoured by the beast. But what could she do? She could make a run for the exit behind her, and could hopefully help free the little boy. But dragons were fast and lethal.

She searched the chamber. Rock and more rock, but none on the ground she could pick up and throw. She may be able to make a dash and grab the torch, but were dragons even afraid of fire? They breathed it.

Her searching eyes caught on the faint gleam of metal resting on a rocky ledge beneath the torch. A sword… She was short, and she hadn't been taught to use a sword, but she would try. She would probably fail, but she would try.

With the dragon distracted, sniffing out its prey behind Maribel, she seized the opportunity and sprinted for the sword. As she grasped the handle, the dragon turned to her, ready for its appetizer.

She hefted the sturdy sword, shuffling her feet to place herself between the dragon and the exit. Standing tall, she firmly planted her feet and forced herself to sound much more courageous than she felt at the moment. "No. Stay away!"

Opening its mouth, it displayed dozens of dagger-sharp teeth, and let out a deafening roar.

Maribel fought her instincts to shrink, to run. She stepped forward, pointing the heavy sword at the dragon's chest in warning. Several panicked voices and screams continued to echo behind her.

The beast crept closer, more smoke billowing from its nostrils.

No matter what, she refused to be intimidated, refused to back down. She too advanced a pace.

Beads of sweat dripped down her neck. The cave was hot, the monster's breath licking against Maribel's skin.

It opened its mouth again, a guttural growl rising as a stream of fire the color of its eyes billowed forth. Maribel charged. Before the blade connected with the dragon's scales, the fire enveloped her.

Gasping, Maribel woke in bed, drenched in sweat. She clawed at her skin, searching for burn marks. There were none. Nonetheless, she ripped off her bedding and stood. Unlatching the window, she yanked it open and sucked in cool, fresh air. The scent of recent rain, despite the bone-dry bushes and grass before her, helped clear the smoke that still lingered in her senses.

It had been *far* too real. Her hands ached as she flexed them. She had gripped the sword like her life had depended on it.

Maribel was jittery all morning, especially at breakfast as she choked down scrambled eggs and passed on the blood orange juice her mother offered. She promptly left the house and made her way to Athena's.

Athena invited her into the backyard, where they could have more privacy.

"That was absolutely mad!" Maribel said. "My hands are killing me."

Athena blew out a breath. "Dragons… Wild. But why are your hands hurting? I … actually don't hurt at all this morning."

Maribel eased herself down on a wooden step of the porch. "From gripping the sword so tightly."

Raising her eyebrows, Athena sat next to her. "You tried to fight it?"

"Yes… Didn't you?"

"I ran away," Athena said.

"Oh." Maribel had known it was a dream at the time, but the lifelike reality had bolstered her determination to save the boy and mother. "That would have been the smart thing to do. I woke covered in sweat."

Athena frowned. "I think I'm done with these dreams."

"Do we even have a choice?"

"Well…" Athena straightened the hem of her skirt. "I mean that when I woke … I didn't smell the rain."

Maribel's heart dropped. They both knew what that meant. Each young maiden who had shared the dreams followed the same pattern. The first morning they woke without the smell of rain would be the end of the dreams, the end of their memories of it ever happening. Athena would sleep normally that night.

She would be better off, too. Who wanted to lose sleep night after night, only to wake in pain? The girls who forgot could go about their regular lives. All but one of Athena and Maribel's friends who had ever experienced the dreams had already forgotten them.

Maribel hugged Athena. "I don't want to do this alone," she confessed. Perhaps there was a way to stop the dreams, but she honestly wasn't sure she wanted to at the moment. They were intriguing, like a puzzle she yearned to piece together.

Athena pulled back from the hug, giving her a smile. "Figure it out. Tell me someday how it all ends, and I promise to believe you."

Smiling in return, Maribel agreed to do just that.

***

Two days later, Maribel was alone. Dozens of maidens around her age had shared the dreams, at least as far as she'd known. They had taken part in the adventure and danger and chaos of it, but she was the only girl she knew who still bore the burden.

She visited Athena again, and explained it all.

"Wow," Athena said in awe. "That sounds exciting! You're sure this happened to me, too?"

Maribel nodded, and Athena shook her head. "It's honestly a little hard to believe, but I've never known you to tell tales…"

"I promise I'm not making it up."

The teakettle whistled from the kitchen, and Athena held up a finger. "I'll be right back."

Minutes later, she returned with tea for them both. "Thanks for visiting. What's on your mind?"

Maribel furrowed her brow. "Just the dreams…"

Athena smiled, taking a sip. "Dreams? What kind of dreams?"

Her jaw dropping, Maribel struggled for words. "The dreams I just told you about…"

"What do you mean?"

She hadn't only forgotten the dreams; she had forgotten being *told* about the dreams just minutes ago. Maribel's heart grew hollow as she pretended nothing was wrong, as they drank tea and chatted about the decidedly dry summer.

As she ambled home that day, Maribel was stumped. This had to be some kind of curse, right? Something that drove people momentarily mad? Some kind of magic that had tainted the rain at the queen's passing, only unleashing itself on a narrow sliver of the population, in semipredictable ways?

When she arrived home, she finally confessed everything to her mother. Her mother eyed her skeptically, and suggested they see a physician.

They weren't five footsteps from the front porch when Maribel voiced her doubts. "I really don't think a physician can do anything about it…" Magic was rare, and she doubted anyone in these parts possessed it.

Her mother paused, clutching her purse. She blinked. "Well, how severe is your neck pain?"

"Like I said, the pain isn't that bad. It's the dreams and everything else."

Frowning, her mother caressed her cheek. "You've been having nightmares?"

A boulder dropped in Maribel's gut, and she kicked herself for hoping it would have somehow been different with her mother. She had already forgotten the primary reason for the physician's visit.

"Yes, nightmares," Maribel replied weakly.

Her mother nodded, still frowning. "I promise we're saving for a new mattress; hopefully that will help. Let's try some chamomile tea this evening to see if it will do the trick."

"Sure."

They abandoned the trip to the physician.

Chapter Five

After eighteen straight nights of these bewildering dreams, Maribel kept chasing the meaning, pondering the purpose during the days as she helped with chores and tried to go about her daily life.

Still fully clueless as to Maribel's plight, Celia dragged her to a couple of shops and then to Athena's for a visit. The usual activities felt so meaningless. Maybe it was simply her loneliness, but Maribel feared there was more at play, that something in her was changing, evolving, emerging in the process.

They wandered the empty pasture behind Athena's home, plucking wildflowers and avoiding the dry old cow chips. "I saw Prince Jonas in his carriage the other day," Athena said, a smile on her lips.

"Any word on his bride?" Celia asked.

Athena shook her head. "No. No one knows. He hasn't said a thing, hasn't been seen with a single girl."

Maribel had been too wrapped up in the mysterious dreams to think of the man. "Maybe he's breaking tradition, and he'll wait a while to take a bride. He's likely still mourning."

Celia arched an eyebrow. "Are you serious? The royal family is blessed to rule. It's tradition and law, and I don't think he would risk breaking either."

Sniffing a fragrant bellflower, Maribel considered. Celia was probably right. And perhaps she should have been thinking about the prince more through this dream ordeal…

This whole thing might be a warning, a premonition about the return of dragons, of society crumbling, of … who knew what disjointed threat the mess of dreams hinted at. What if Maribel was the last person to still remember, and then her memories vanished like all the others?

It was a bone-chilling thought. And what if it wasn't a premonition? What if it was the beginning of an attack by a neighboring kingdom's sorcerer? There hadn't been war in these parts in centuries, and maybe mankind was due for another.

"How does one get an audience with the prince?" Maribel asked.

Celia and Athena smirked in unison.

"Going to offer yourself as his bride?" Athena kidded.

"If you do, please go in something pink or purple, not green," Celia pleaded.

Exasperated, Maribel rolled her eyes. "I'm not planning on throwing myself at him."

She let it go as they wandered the field and gossiped.

A half hour later, she made an excuse to walk home alone. Celia stayed behind with Athena again.

Kicking pebbles out of her path, Maribel seriously reconsidered the idea of approaching the prince. Her heart sank. If he somehow didn't find her mad, he'd forget with his next breath what she'd told him, just like everyone else. She was a lower-middle-class commoner, too, and may not be granted an audience with him. Though, the queen had been much lower in station than even Maribel when the king had selected her as his bride, so hopefully the prince didn't look down on the poor, not when his mother had once been.

An idea sparked in Maribel's mind as she straightened. Maybe he already knew what was going on, knew about this looming magical threat. Perhaps that was why he hadn't been seen courting any maidens. He was too busy.

She smiled as she recalled how regal he always looked. He would be a good king. He would take care of his people. She would like to meet him someday.

Rubbing her lower back—her current pain of the day from a dream where she'd single-handedly rolled boulders in front of a flooding stream—she convinced herself that if this was indeed some type of threat, the prince was probably already on top of it.

*****

Invisible rain claimed her once again that night. Maribel's eyelids fluttered. Her balance wavered as she took in the scene around her, her heart beating wildly.

She stood atop a small platform floating high above a raging river. She gulped as she glanced over her shoulders. The edge of a canyon loomed far behind her, with no way in sight to reach it.

The only exit from the platform was a narrow stone path directly in front of her, only wide enough to place one foot at a time.

Her short height would probably help with her balance, her lower center of gravity useful as she would work her way across the path, but it was *so* high up here. She was afraid of heights, and the water below was far from welcoming.

She squared her shoulders. These tasks often terrified her, but they also made her feel alive.

Out of nowhere, an invisible hand, soft and warm, large and strong, grasped her left hand. She searched for the owner, but there was none. The hand squeezed hers, bolstering her courage as she took the first step.

She loosed a breath, then placed the next foot forward. Her invisible companion helped improve her balance, step after step, as the torrent writhed far below.

The path was straight, narrow as a balance beam. Each footstep was slow and intentional. Had she been an acrobat, it wouldn't have taken her so long to cross, but she played to her strengths, and that of the imaginary help the dream had provided.

After a painstakingly long time on the beam, she reached the end, her hand still firmly held by … no one. She stood on another small platform, but had not quite reached the other edge of the canyon. There was no path forward. Only a terrifying gap for her short legs to try to jump across.

Her breath shaky, she kept looking between the edge and the water below.

"I can't swim well," she whispered. With that far of a drop, she likely wouldn't even survive to try swimming if she fell.

The warm hand squeezed again. "You can do this," a voice whispered back. The voice was masculine, kind and reassuring, from where the man's face might have been had the hand belonged to a real person.

Maribel's heart thundered in her chest. "I…"

"You can do this," the voice whispered again.

"Okay." She sucked in a breath, reminding herself it was only a dream. She wouldn't *actually* die if she fell… Right?

She held the hand tightly. "One… Two…" She crouched. "Three!" She lunged for the edge of the canyon, and the phantom hand released hers right before she landed on the other side on her stomach.

Before she could thank the imaginary hand, she woke in bed to the aroma of fresh rain, a smile on her lips. Her thighs quivered from the exertion of having to balance so carefully for so long. She hadn't even noticed how much they'd burned during the dream, not with the loud river below, not with her focus on the path and the man's hand.

As it was still early morning, she closed her eyes to get more sleep. This time as she nodded off, no rain accompanied her rest, but she kept a smile on her face. She hadn't had a beau for some time.

She would like to have a man hold her again, though more than just holding her hand.

***

Nineteen nights. Nineteen nights in a row had been spent in rain-kissed dreams. Maribel genuinely couldn't tell if she dreaded this pattern continuing, or if she looked forward to it at this point. If it was part of some greater threat, it wasn't a very good one…

She challenged herself to simply enjoy the day and try not to analyze the situation. It was sunny, and she needed to get out of the house.

After breakfast, she called on Celia, and they strolled to the library together. The library was one of the biggest buildings in town.

After an hour perusing books to borrow, they hefted bags full of novels to take home. Maribel's selections focused on dreams, dragons, and magic. She'd tried to remind herself she was taking a day off from the mystery, so she'd wait until the next day to start reading them.

"Less than two weeks before the coronation—and before we find out who he chose as his bride," Celia said, changing which hand she carried her books with.

Maribel smiled. "I hope he chooses well, and I hope he's happy." If the prince took after his parents, he would be kind and wise, and deserved the best.

As Maribel settled into bed that night, she thought of Prince Jonas, and she mulled over her own life. He was facing a big decision, and stepping into big shoes as he ascended the throne and selected a life partner. Maribel's decisions weren't as weighty as his, but she still needed to sort out her future. She didn't have a deadline for marriage, but she wouldn't turn a man down, providing he was the right one.

Before she knew it, familiar rain rocked her to sleep. Opening her eyes, she was blinded by white. She'd never seen anything like it before.

The room—presuming it *was* a room—had no visible corners, walls, windows, ceiling, anything. It was just blank whiteness. There were no tasks she could discern. Was she supposed to find a way out?

A knock sounded behind her, and she whipped around. "Hello?"

"Are you dressed?" a male voice asked.

She furrowed her brow. "What?"

"Are you dressed?" he repeated.

She glanced down at her nightgown. "Um… Yes…" It was a little odd to be in her nightgown. The dreams had usually dressed her in something appropriate for the adventure each night.

An ornate wooden door appeared, the golden knob twisting. In strode an elegant man, his hands clasped before him. Not just any man—Prince Jonas.

Maribel's brain stuttered. "I… Hello… Your Highness?" She curtsied.

He gave her a single nod, closing the door behind him. It vanished into the canvas of white. He said nothing, simply observing her.

"I…" She cocked her head. "You're… I mean … this isn't any different, right? Of course it's not. I mean you're not. I mean…" She tried to calm her racing mind, her rambling. He wasn't actually here. None of the people had *really* been in her dreams.

Her eyes widened. "You're not dead, are you? Because my schoolteacher…"

The prince's lips twitched into a smile. "No, I'm not dead."

"Good. That would be bad. Obviously… Just making sure. But…" She arched an eyebrow. "Would a dream know if the real person inspiring the dream was alive or dead?"

Amusement danced in his eyes, his smile growing wider. "I suppose not for most people…"

"Okay." She blinked, trying to wrap her head around the logic and mystery.

Prince Jonas kept surveying her. "What's your name?"

She pointed to herself. "Me?"

He chuckled. "You're the only other person here."

"Yes, but I'm not accustomed to introducing myself in my own dreams." She swallowed, her mouth dry. Why was he so handsome? "I'm Maribel."

His eyes were the color of freshly shucked peas from the garden, though they sparkled like the night sky. "That's a beautiful name."

She smiled. "Thank you."

"And a nice smile to match." His voice was so smooth. Did he sound like that in real life? She'd only heard a grief-stricken version of him at his mother's funeral.

"Sorry about your mother," she said. It was silly to offer condolences to a figment of her imagination, but it felt right.

As real as anything in the other dreams, his expression was solemn as he nodded. "Thank you. I had good parents." He paused. "What of yours? Tell me about yourself and your family."

At ease and grateful to not be completing an arduous task, she sat on the cool white floor. He followed suit a couple of feet in front of her.

She went on and on, sharing her story. How her parents were kind, her younger siblings fun but annoying, as any siblings should be. He found that comment particularly humorous.

Prince Jonas nodded and took it all in as she explained her family's situation, her childhood, and even talked about her friends. He didn't once grimace or cringe in judgment. Then again, why would he? He was her, after all. He was a figment of her imagination, something a strange magical sleep had created.

Part of her wished he could be more as she bared her soul to him, as he nodded and asked the occasional clarifying question.

She even explained the weird dreams, and he didn't seem to think her mad. He offered a few comments to assure her there was no magical threat at play.

After what had to be hours, she'd caught him up on all the important details. He hadn't shared as much about himself as she had, but she'd loved the tidbits he'd given her. He enjoyed botany, and long hikes with his hound—Wesley—and experimented in the castle's kitchens at times. Everyone in the kingdom knew about Wesley, but the other details must have been something Maribel's imagination made up.

A part of her heart yearned for him to be the real man. He made her comfortable. He felt like a friend. A dashing, handsome, sweet, eligible friend...

She adjusted her seat, making sure her nightgown covered her knees. "I want to know more about you. Or... You know, the real Prince Jonas. Would you *actually* know anything about him? Or since this is a dream, you really only know what I already know?"

Ever calm and smooth, he replied, "I suppose that depends on what you know of the man. You'd like to meet him?"

Her cheeks warmed as she averted her gaze. "I think most maidens in the kingdom would be interested in meeting him."

"I didn't ask about most maidens."

She cleared her throat, locking eyes with him. "Yes. I think that would be exciting, but at least I got this dream."

While she'd fancied him, she'd never once imagined herself baking a cake beside him in the castle's kitchens, or hiking with him and his hound. But now she could, and she'd be terribly sad to remember this conversation with no hopes of it ever coming true.

Prince Jonas drew a deep breath, standing. She stood as well.

He straightened his jacket. Unlike Maribel, he wore full formal clothing, not nightclothes. "I like you, Maribel," he said. "Come find me."

Blinking, she couldn't believe her ears. "What? I... What? Will I get to see the castle in this dream?"

He strode for the wooden door that again appeared before him. Opening it, he turned to her, smiling. "Come find me." Without another word, he passed through the door, and it closed behind him.

She hadn't been able to make out the task of the night, but the only way out was through the door he'd just exited. She grabbed the handle, swinging the door open.

Her eyes shot open as she lay in bed. She soon found her bearings.

Sitting up, she drew a breath, then frowned. *No rain.*

She had to have done something wrong, or the spell or curse or whatever it was had been dispelled. She wanted to go back to figure it out, but there was no door, no white room.

Come find me, his voice whispered in her mind. *Come find me.*

Standing, she wrapped her arm around a bedpost. She couldn't just march up to the castle. She'd never been there, and the madness of a dream didn't permit her entrance to his residence in the middle of the night. Unlike most of the other dreams, she'd woken from this one while it was still pitch-black outside.

Come find me, his lingering beckon whispered, softer than before.

"Where?" she whispered back into the void of her bedroom.

A map bloomed in her mind, a path to a park across town.

Adventure called, and her heart swelled. She was going to be mad enough to answer that call.

She'd been to that park before, though she'd never snuck out in the middle of the night. Nor had these feverish dreams ever called to her when she was awake, but she couldn't resist the challenge.

She glanced at her nightgown and stripped it off, taking a minute to change into a dress. If she was found roaming the streets like a crazed person at all hours, she at least ought to look civilized… Smiling, she plucked up her favorite green ribbon and tied it around her waist, high with a nice bow, so as to match the current fashion. It looked nice against the backdrop of cream fabric. She ran a brush through her hair, then paused.

This couldn't be real. There was absolutely no way the real prince would be at that park in the middle of the night. As she set her brush down, her heart faltered a little. It wasn't real. She was being a fool. She was exhausted from twenty nights straight spent in feverish dreams.

A deep gouge on the wooden vanity claimed her focus, and she ran a finger over it. That scratch had been there as long as she could remember. Had her previous dreams been so vivid? None of them had been set in her present surroundings, in her own home…

Her heart warmed as she recollected Prince Jonas's fetching smile. He wouldn't be at the park. But she would never forgive herself if she didn't check to see.

Not owning a sword, and not being skilled with one—as evidenced by the dragon dream—she instead strapped on the dagger her father had bought her for safety. She may be making questionable choices at the moment, but she wasn't completely daft. Before exiting her room, she scratched out a quick letter to explain where she'd gone.

Chapter Six

As she tiptoed down the hallway, only a single floorboard creaked to scold her. She held her breath but made her way out the front door without waking anyone.

The night was cool and clear, the crickets softly singing their song. Maribel beamed. *I'm on my way.*

She didn't trust herself on horseback in the dark, and no public coaches ran the streets at this time of night, so she traveled on foot, aiming for every shortcut she knew. She ran across a bridge, weaved through streets and back roads, and rounded a small pond.

Eventually, the park lay before her, and Maribel hesitated. This was all the mental map—the vision—had shown. It was a fairly large park, too… She surveyed the area. To one side towered a giant tree— a weeping willow—that had been framed within the image.

Her feet tired, she strode for the tree. The trunk was dark under the dense curtain of leaves blocking out the moonlight. As she approached the tree, rustling startled her, and she halted. "Hello?" She cautiously slid a hand to her concealed dagger.

"Maribel," he said. "You came." The voice matched that of Prince Jonas, at least the version she'd just met in her dream.

"Is this ... still a dream?" she asked as a warm rain began to mist above her. She'd never had a dream within a dream, but perhaps that was what this was. She glanced toward the skies as the rain picked up. Hadn't it been a clear night?

"Come in from the rain," he beckoned.

She did not want to test the thickness of her dress's cream fabric when wet—dream or not. She ducked beneath the willow's branches, and beheld the prince. "Is it really you?"

His smile was swoonworthy. "Yes. Is it really you?"

"Well… Yes." She forgot her manners but quickly recovered, curtsying. "Your Highness."

He folded his arms, leaning against the tree's sturdy trunk. "You don't have to curtsy to me. And you can call me Jonas."

Nervous, she fidgeted with her hands. "I'm not so sure about that. You're the prince. You'll soon be my king." She still wasn't completely sure this was real.

"I'll be offended if you call me by my title."

"Okay… Jonas…" It didn't feel unnatural to utter it.

He grinned. "My name sounds good on your lips."

Her stomach flipped. Everything sounded good so far on *his* lips. She dared to take a step forward. "Did you have a dream that brought you here?" If this was somehow real, how had he known to meet here, in the middle of the night, if he hadn't shared the dream? How had he known her name?

"In a way. I was in *your* dream."

She had so many questions, because he didn't seem fazed by any of this. "Why?"

"Because that's how the selection process works, darling."

Darling? Her heart skipped a beat. And then she put together what he'd said. He couldn't be serious… "When you say 'selection process'…"

Jonas cocked his head. "I think you know."

What did he need to select in the next few days if not a bride? "I'm not queen material!"

He searched her eyes in silence for a moment. "Aren't you? You respected the power and legacy that came before you by observing my mother's passing, by standing in the rain that day. You've completed twenty nights of dreams designed to test you, to find you. With each test, you proved yourself worthy. You were kind, strong, loyal, and brave. Forgiving and clever. Well-educated."

She gaped. She'd told him about the dreams, but not every detail. "There are girls who are smarter, prettier, wiser…"

"But they're not you."

She couldn't believe his casual insistence. "I would have been killed trying to slay a dragon like an idiot!"

He chuckled, a sweet melody to her ears. "Brave, for being willing to risk your life to save others. Clever, for finding the best path to stop the flooding. Kind, by helping a beggar." He rattled off a virtue for each of her tests. "And frankly, darling, no single person can take down a dragon alone with a simple blade. I certainly didn't during my trial."

"But I *knew* I was in a dream, that I wouldn't actually get hurt." She bobbed her head. The dreams had been astonishingly real, and *had* actually hurt her each time, though not much. "You can't choose someone to rule the kingdom with you based on how they act in a dream."

Shifting his weight, Jonas nodded. "Perhaps not in a regular dream. But in an enchanted dream, you are yourself. The most honest and raw version of yourself. For generations, the dream trials have selected correctly. You didn't prepare for them, or put on a face for me, didn't plot or plan to win a prize."

"Isn't that what you just did, though? Put me through twenty nights of tests to show I'm worthy of being your bride? Your prize?"

He winced. "First of all, Maribel, *I* didn't put you through it. The royal family is full of dreamers. As the heavens mourned my mother's passing, as her magic was released into the world, *it* began the process to find you." He paused. "And you weren't alone in your trials. I have also had to face dreams each night."

Maribel furrowed her brow. He *had* just mentioned that he'd faced a dragon during *his* trial… "But you rule by birthright. What do you have to prove?"

"True. Not all our trials were the same. Most were different, in fact. Mine were not to select me, but to refine and prepare me to be a worthy ruler, a good husband, a kind … father, someday."

She swallowed. *One step at a time…* There were so many maidens out there, and she still couldn't believe it was her he'd called here this night. But it made sense with what she'd witnessed. Several women within her own acquaintance had experienced the first dreams, and the numbers had thinned down each night. "How many girls made it all the way through?"

"You. There is no one else."

She couldn't breathe. "I didn't sign up for it. I… What of your preferences? And mine? And *love?* Maybe I passed a few tests, but shouldn't there be something more?"

Jonas bit his lip. "The magic takes preferences into account. It knows your heart and desires, and mine as well. And you could have ended the dreams at any time. You could have refused to answer the schoolteacher, could have asked others in the dreams how to stop them." He searched her eyes, his expression soft. "And what is love, if not mutual respect, a willingness to work on shared goals, and attraction?"

Attraction? Surely he wanted someone taller, thinner, with straighter teeth, or whose hair didn't frizz in the humidity like hers no doubt was with the rain still pounding down on the leaves and branches above them. "Are you … attracted to me? There are plenty of maidens more beautiful."

His eyes traced her from head to toe, devouring her entirely as a smirk tugged on his lips. "I did get to finally see you in tonight's dream, did I not? I got to know you, and see you. And I asked you to come."

Her heart thundered.

"Do you dislike what you know of me? What you've seen of me?" he asked.

Her knees weakened. "I, uh…" she breathed. No, she didn't at all dislike anything she'd ever learned about him or witnessed. Not a single part of his devastatingly handsome self. "You're … handsome."

He angled his head. "I enjoyed learning about you tonight. But I don't expect an answer right away. My coronation is in a week and a half. We can get to know each other before you decide. I'd like you to spend time with me in my home. You'll have your own room."

She was all nerves. "And if I don't agree to marry you?"

"Then…" His tone held hesitation. "I'll have no choice but to select a maiden at random. I don't imagine I'd be as happy, or that the kingdom would thrive as much, but it's your choice to make. And we wouldn't have to wed right away. We would have a full year. I only have to announce my *intentions*, and *present* you at my coronation."

She had so many questions, so much anxiety. What of her family and friends?

"The public still won't remember the dreams, just like you won't, should you choose to reject the magic's matching. But I'll invite your family to the castle tomorrow if you like, to discuss the matter."

I might forget this all happened? A frown overtook her lips. She didn't want to forget any of it. As intense as some of the trials had been, and despite how lonely she'd felt at times, she wouldn't trade any of these memories, wouldn't give them up without a fight. And he had been so sweet and charming during the dream just a couple of hours ago, and now as he waited to hear what he hoped for…

Fear. Fear held her back. "I don't know anything about defending a kingdom against a threat. Or proper court manners, or *anything* a queen would need to know."

He smiled confidently. "I was raised for this. I'll teach you."

"I still have nothing to offer but my heart and life. And I want more than to be a checklist wife and mother to heirs."

"Is that what you think my parents' union was like?" His eyebrows knit. "Theirs is the closest, most equal relationship I've ever seen."

She hadn't meant it like that. And she'd never heard anything negative about the pair.

"I would never force you to have my children, Maribel. If it came to it, and we never had children, my cousin would rule after we both pass. And…" He ran a hand through his hair, frustration showing. "You have *a lot* to contribute." He paused, softening. "This is the way it's done. This kingdom was established on the principle of balance. My mother was dirt poor. My father's father before him was also a commoner. The ruling family has *always* selected a commoner. The *magic* has always selected a commoner to help guide the dreamer born with royal blood. You keep us grounded. I've never experienced your life. You could help me understand my own people better. You can see things where my life of privilege may keep me blind. Don't say you have nothing of value to offer."

He was passionate. And she didn't hate a single word that came from his mouth. She swallowed, taking a step forward. "Will you teach me to dance? Because I don't know the right steps for a proper ball."

He smiled once again. "I would love nothing more. But you have to promise me something first…"

"What's that?"

"I take it you're not that shy, from our conversation earlier tonight."

She shrugged. "Not really."

"Then you can teach me that, too. I … struggle to know how to easily converse with strangers."

It was comical how innocently he'd said it, and also how untrue it was. "You haven't once hesitated to talk with me tonight. You're not shy."

He opened his mouth, but nothing came out for a moment. "I can give official speeches just fine. And I don't have a problem talking to *you*, because I feel like I'm talking to an old friend. Strangers are different."

Her heart melted on the spot. He felt like an old friend as well. An astoundingly attractive one, who she was somehow only a couple of paces from now… "I'll see what I can do."

"So, you'll come home with me?" he asked. "To the castle. Get to know me, and make your decision?"

His lips begged to be kissed. The castle sounded wonderful. Dancing… All of it. Why did she hesitate?

"I'm still nervous," she confessed.

Jonas held out a hand, and she met him in the middle, resting hers in his. His hand was soft and warm, large and strong, familiar as it enveloped hers. In the most gentle, soothing voice, he said, "You can do this."

Her eyes wide, she gasped. How had she not recognized that voice instantly? Or the hand now wrapped around hers? "You were in my dream last night too?"

He smiled brightly. "The first time I got to hear your voice, got to feel you. If I'm honest, that pep talk was half for me, because I'm also not a great swimmer, nor am I fond of heights. But we walked that precarious path together, didn't we?"

He had given her the courage and stability she'd needed to complete it. The boost she'd needed to take a literal leap of faith.

She stared into his handsome green eyes as his thumb stroked the back of her hand. "Let's give this a chance."

Jonas sucked in a breath. "Thank you."

They shared a smile, still standing there. Had she really just accepted the prince's request to court her? To possibly become his bride?

Maribel swallowed again. "How far is it from here to the castle?"

"Not far, considering I have a carriage waiting at the other end of the park." He lifted his free hand, tucking her damp hair behind her ear. "I know I've already asked a lot of you tonight, but will you do me one more favor?"

"What?"

His lips twitched, whether out of mischief or embarrassment she wasn't sure.

"You're breathtaking in that cream dress, but I'm trying to be a proper ruler, not a scoundrel of a prince. And as much as I would like to see through that dress, we shouldn't test the fortitude of the fabric in this rain."

Her cheeks warmed at his bluntness, her heart pounding as much as the rainstorm above.

"You can stop the rain," he said.

Maribel scoffed. "I don't have magic. I can't control the weather."

He drew her in, sliding a hand to her waist, gently holding her chin. "You won't get the dreamer's magic until we wed, but you *can* stop this rain. Only you and I can stop *this* rain, because it was enchanted this whole time for us."

The day of the queen's passing, every night surrounding Maribel's enchanted dreams, and the moment she had arrived at the park and he'd called to her from under this tree…

His eyes held nothing but desire, and it ignited something new in her as she savored his touch. She stretched tall as he leaned forward, their lips grazing in absolute perfection.

And the downpour *instantly* stopped.

She pulled back, shocked. The dark night was still. "We actually did that?"

Laughing, he nodded. "I would never lie to you, darling."

That kiss… "If we… If we kissed again, would it turn back on?"

"No, but we could kiss again if you're worried it will, just to be safe. Just to ensure it doesn't start again and flood the kingdom." He winked.

The butterflies in her stomach took flight anew. He was a magnet she imagined might always draw her in. Standing on tiptoe and wrapping her arms around his neck, she smiled. "If I might be the queen, I feel it's my duty to do everything I can to prevent a natural disaster like that."

A heartbeat later, they savored another kiss, or a dozen… When did one kiss start and another end? It was dizzying as his lips caressed hers time and time again, as every part of her melted in his arms, as her mind turned to putty.

Jonas was the first to pull back, panting. "We should… It's late. Or early… We should get some rest before daylight, don't you think?"

It was the wise thing to do. "Yes." She wanted more in the moment, so much more, more than she'd ever wanted from a man. But she would be wise. "I'll, uh, still have my own room?"

He exuded that same passion, continuing to hold her against him. But like a gentleman, he lifted her hand, kissing it. "For as long as you desire."

Forcing herself to peel away, she straightened her dress, blowing out a cooling breath. "Yes. Let's sleep on this. Separately." She grasped his extended hand, and they emerged from the cover of the tree. Her cheeks warm at what she'd just done, what she'd just agreed to, she was embarrassed, but not ashamed. His hand held hers so naturally. His heart accepted hers so easily.

The carriage driver greeted them and opened the door. Jonas helped Maribel up, then sat beside her on the bench. It was nicer than any coach or carriage she'd been in before. Every part of her wanted to be on Jonas's lap, wanted to be all over him. Never had she connected with someone so deeply, so quickly. She'd only kissed one other beau before, and what she'd just shared with Jonas was nothing like the time she'd let the blacksmith's son stick his tongue down her throat.

There truly was magic in the match. Somehow, she doubted she'd need to take the full week and a half to consider his proposal, but chemistry was only part of the equation. She willed herself to stay on her side of the bench as the carriage jostled forward.

Jonas reached down, rubbing the end of the green ribbon she'd used as a decorative belt. "I like this," he said. "I like green. It reminds me of spring, and all things happy and fresh."

She suppressed a giggle. "It's my favorite color."

His own green gaze settled on her with what she could only describe as bedroom eyes. She took a sharp breath. "So, I want to hear everything about you. Every story, goal, allergy… Everything. Don't leave anything out."

He gave her a toothy smile, resting his hand on her knee. "Where should we start?"

Chapter Seven

Maribel soaked up everything about Jonas on the ride to the castle. He was sweet, and passionate about his calling as the soon-to-be king. Wesley the hound instantly became a new friend upon their arrival. A messenger was dispatched to her home with word of her whereabouts so her family wouldn't worry. Servants didn't hesitate to see to her needs regarding toiletries and a nightgown—a luxurious silky one far above the quality her family could have ever afforded.

The mattress in her chambers was as soft as a cloud, her rest as perfect and still as she'd had before the enchanted rain had taken her on this journey. Just a few hours later, she woke, a little worn from an eventful night, but happy. With a smile on her face, she took in the elegant room.

She blinked, making sure it was real. She was sleeping in the castle, almost engaged to the prince himself. How had that just happened? Her smile widened as she replayed the long conversations they'd held—in the dream, under the tree, and in the carriage. Her heart warmed even more at the memory of the kiss he'd given her as he'd bid her goodnight. Those eyes… Those lips…

Getting out of bed, she readied for the day, excited for the adventure ahead.

The next week was a whirlwind, and Maribel didn't regret a moment of it. Her admiration for Jonas grew by the hour as he held her in his arms for dance lessons to prepare for his coronation, as he taught her what it would mean to be his queen, to be a queen of the people. He invited her family to the castle for a visit, and even Celia. Maribel wasn't able to share the secret of the match, the sacred magic of the dreamers within the royal family, but they were happy for her.

She was a little surprised Celia took the news so well. In the end, Celia's jealousy didn't get the better of her; she was excited to be at the castle, and ecstatic at the prospect of visiting her best friend often for royal gossip and luxurious balls.

The couple explained they'd agreed to keep their courtship a secret until now, and her loved ones were none the wiser, assuming *that* was what she'd really been doing the last few weeks when she'd been running around trying to sort out the mystery of the dreams.

At the end of that week, with just a couple of days left before his coronation, before he had to announce his bride, she accepted, and didn't look back for a moment. They had been matched by the magic, had fought their own dragons, had navigated their own pains and dreams to be worthy of each other, to be worthy of the people they would serve as a team.

Maribel had needed to sort out her life as a new adult, but she hadn't pushed herself yet. Perhaps fate had known all along what her life had been preparing her for…

***

Maribel strolled through Jonas's chambers, out to his private balcony the night before his coronation, before he presented her publicly as his betrothed. She was still getting used to the heavy ring he'd given her.

She spotted him stargazing on a soft bench. "There you are."

He instantly grinned, scooting to make room for her. She eased down, cuddling up to him.

"Hello, darling."

Why did she love it so much when he called her that? "Sorry it took so long." She'd just been with the tailor for a last-minute fitting for her custom ball gown. "But I'll admit, it's rather nice having someone who fits clothes to your size and shape, and not having to shop around."

"The best for the best," he said.

"Hmm…" She twisted her lips. "That could come across as classist…"

He turned, arching an eyebrow. "Because I think you're amazing, and I plan to spoil you?"

She poked his arm. "Because it could sound like only those in power deserve the finest quality of clothing—the best fabrics, and cuts to properly fit their body."

Jonas cocked his head, considering. "I certainly didn't intend it that way, but I see what you mean… Putting me in my place before we're even wed…" He winked.

Maribel beamed. "Isn't that why you picked me?"

His gaze flickered to her lips, then back to her eyes. "I picked you for many reasons. And I still defend that you're the best, and I intend to give you the best. And I can't wait to see you in that dress tomorrow."

"I'll take it." She snuck a kiss. "Are you nervous about tomorrow?"

He blew out a breath, and they chatted awhile. From the moment he'd walked into her dream, and even before that when he'd held her hand on the precipice, he had felt like a companion to her soul. They would always share moments like this.

It was getting late, and they both ought to go to bed to be fresh for the big day. The attention of thousands would be on them both. But she lingered longer in his arms on that cozy bench, soaking it in.

A smile tugged at her lips. "You know, when we have children…" In their unending hours together, they'd agreed that they both *did* want them down the road. "They'll have the dreamer gift, and they'll be privy to the knowledge of the process…"

"Yes…"

"So, I'll make it a point to let them know their father was a royal pain." She considered the tests she'd had to pass. "You were a pain in the neck, a pain in the backside…" she kidded.

Jonas chuckled, then grazed her ear with his lips. "Okay, but you have to promise me you'll also tell them one other important thing…"

She leaned into his touch. "What's that?"

His whisper was soft and sensual. "Make sure to also tell them I was the man of your dreams."

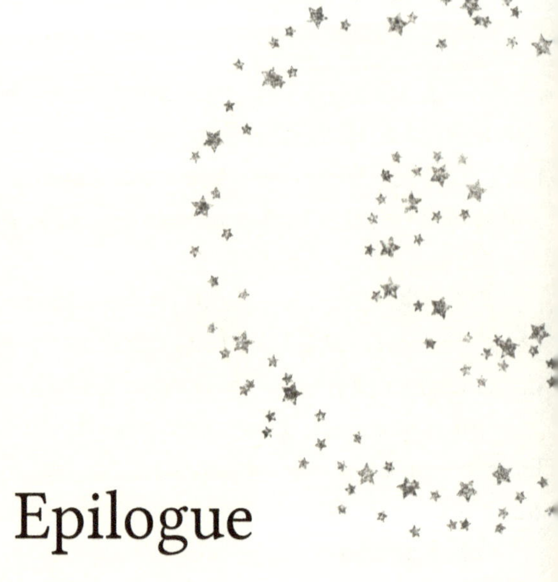

Epilogue

Jonas's coronation was less than an hour away. Maribel sat in her own dressing room as servants fussed over last-minute touches on her hair and dress. She tried to tackle the day a minute at a time, a breath at a time.

A soft tap sounded on the door, and a servant opened it.

"Okay if I come in?" Jonas asked.

"Yes," Maribel replied. As Jonas walked in, she stood and turned.

Stunned and speechless, he gaped. Jonas's eyes swept up and down the elegant green gown she wore. He was well-decorated too.

"Darling," he finally breathed.

She couldn't stop smiling. If he was this stunned to see her in this coronation-day ball gown, what would his reaction be on their wedding day?

"You look handsome," she said as the servants silently slipped out of the room, shutting the door behind them.

"And you…" His throat bobbed.

She loved him, absolutely loved him. "Please tell me I won't be too distracting as you take your title today."

He cleared his throat, grinning. "I'll manage. It's a shame we don't have more time, and that you've already applied lipstick, though."

Her stomach flipped. "How about a hug before they drag us apart?"

Swooping in, he took her advice, holding her tight.

"You'll make a fantastic king," she said.

"Mmm. And you'll make a fantastic queen when you're ready." He stepped back, caressing her cheek. "You're sure you want to do this? It's not always an easy life."

She *had* reconsidered the original agreement they'd made just a couple of days ago. "I was actually thinking…"

His look was hesitant, worried.

She fiddled with a shiny button on his jacket. "What if we moved up the wedding? A year is an awfully long time to wait…"

Pure joy bloomed on his face. "Really? We ought to stick to whatever I announce today, so if you have any doubts…"

"I have zero doubts."

His eyes searched hers. "When are you thinking?"

She wrapped her arms around him, whispering in his ear.

Shocked but excited, he leaned back. "You're sure?"

Maribel nodded. "Absolutely."

Minutes later, servants guided Maribel to an alcove, where she sat alone for the coronation ceremony, just a few yards from the platform Jonas would soon stand on. This day was primarily about Jonas ascending the throne, and she was happy to keep that focus on him until he announced who his betrothed was.

The alcove was angled in such a way that the thousands of spectators who came to the head church couldn't see her. Her family and closest friends had special seats, though.

Her anticipation was overflowing, her nerves building as she waited, as the church rustled with movement and hushed gossip.

A gong rang, and the whispers silenced, followed by the rustle of thousands of people standing, Maribel included.

Jonas was the picture of regality as he walked into the room. He kept his eyes forward, meeting his people head-on, save the quick glance toward her alcove. Her heart skipped a beat, and his lips twitched ever so slightly.

When he reached the spot appointed for him, he halted and bowed to the people. They sat again, and with the guidance of the head clergyman, Jonas took his oath. He promised absolute loyalty—his life and time—to his people.

He and Maribel had spent every spare moment together since her selection. He'd shared the trials the dreams had presented him. Maribel's smile grew as she reflected on them, and on how he would truly do good, how he would leave a strong legacy for his children someday. How they both would for *their* children someday. And his magic was *powerful.* Far more powerful than she could have fathomed from simple dreams. He didn't take his gift or position lightly.

Maribel's heart nearly burst with pride as Jonas kneeled, and the clergyman placed a new crown upon his head. As Jonas stood, the people cheered, and Maribel fought pooling tears. He spared her another glance before stepping forward to address his people.

"Thank you for coming to celebrate a new day, a new age for this beautiful kingdom. I am honored to be your king. I will do everything in my power to serve you, to keep peace and prosperity within our borders and with our neighbors." He really did speak with power and authority, even if he was a bit shy in private.

"I am blessed by birthright to inherit this position, but I have done everything I can to prepare myself, and will continue to do so. You loved my parents; they served you justly. I offer no less than they did. And I can assure you your future queen will also be a great asset to our people."

Maribel's stomach twisted as he gave her a small smile, as all eyes rested on the alcove they knew she sat in. Part of her would be happy to let Jonas keep the spotlight, but she wouldn't back down. The magic had picked her, and so had Jonas, and she had picked him and this position.

Jonas continued. "Would you like to meet your future queen?"

The people cheered almost as loudly as they had when celebrating their new king. Sweating, Maribel stood, straightening her dress. She was really going to do this. *They* were going to do this.

He held out his hand, beckoning her. Maribel took a deep breath, and stepped out, his hand a guide to keep her path true. Thousands of eyes rested upon her, hushed whispers no doubt assessing her. She kept her eyes on Jonas, their smiles growing in unison until she reached him.

Just like in her nineteenth dream, his hand was strong and warm, reassuring as it took hers. He lifted her hand to his lips, not breaking eye contact. Her knees weakened. That look, those vibrant green eyes, got her every time.

Jonas again turned to his people, wrapping an arm around Maribel. She always loved the balance his parents had portrayed in public—official, formal, but not stuffy. The people knew there was genuine affection between the king and queen.

"This is Lady Maribel, your future queen."

The crowd bowed, then continued to take her in. The change of power was a time of uncertainty. This kingdom had been blessed with righteous rulers for generations, in part because of the dreamer magic and the enchanted selection process, though the people didn't know about those. But they had to be curious about a new king and queen. Jonas had made public appearances as the prince, though not nearly as many as he could have. Maribel would help him overcome his shyness in more intimate gatherings. She, however, had been plucked from obscurity, and the people had to be more skeptical of her.

Her friends and family beamed, though. Her parents and younger siblings sat on a front-row bench—all dressed in sharp, fitted brand-new clothing for the ceremony. Next to them sat Celia donning a pink dress, and Athena in a wine-red dress.

"Lady Maribel is like no other," Jonas said. "Her love for this kingdom and loyalty to it are unmatched. She is quick-witted, and excited to learn more about matters of state. Just as she has won my heart, she will win yours."

They shared another glance, and she didn't care if thousands of people watched them, analyzed them.

"We've appreciated the privacy we've been allowed during our courtship," he said.

Maribel hid a smirk. Even to her friends and family, the story would always be that they had casually met in town, that they'd courted in secret. The details had always been vague when a future king or queen took their commoner spouse. Only the castle's servants knew she'd been there for a mere ten days, and hadn't stepped foot on those grounds before then. But in those dreams, in that magic match, in the hours upon hours of time they'd spent with each other over the past ten days, she and Jonas had gotten to know each other well. Not a speck of doubt lay in her heart or mind about this choice.

Jonas went on to introduce Maribel, providing details about her family, what part of the kingdom she was from, what her interests and talents were. Looks in the crowd slowly shifted from curiosity to warm acceptance. Some of them had likely wanted to be picked, or to have their daughters picked, and felt slighted that they had never been given the opportunity. But they all had. Every single one of the available maidens around Maribel and Jonas's ages had had equal opportunity; they just would not remember because of the rain's magic.

After introducing her, Jonas nodded for Maribel to speak. They'd practiced their speeches, and despite that and her certainty of this choice, her hands went clammy. She'd never stood in front of a crowd like this, had never given such a public speech, but she had to start somewhere as the king's betrothed. His hand on her back gave her more courage.

"I'd like to say how honored I am to stand next to our king, and for the trust you place in me as your future queen. His Majesty is a good man with a warm heart. He has great pride in his people, as do I."

She wanted to address why she'd been chosen over anyone else, but she couldn't get into those details, and it wasn't the right place or time. She *knew* she was lucky, but that she had also *earned* her place there, in part because she was the type of girl to strive to always be worthy of the trust placed in her. She wasn't *better* than all the other maidens, just more suited to the position, and more compatible with Jonas.

Maribel stood tall, making sure her posture was confident. "We look forward to getting to know you more, and to celebrating our union with you all." She glanced back up at Jonas.

He threw her a questioning look, and she nodded. She was sure in her choice to move up the wedding. She wouldn't advise her friends or siblings to consent to marry someone they'd only met a few days ago, or to wed them so quickly, but her situation was far from typical. Magic was rare, and there had been magic in the match.

Jonas held her hand, facing the audience. "We invite you to attend our wedding in six months' time."

Excited chatter broke out. Jonas had been required to pick a bride by today, and announce her. The law also required he marry within a year of taking the throne.

The couple didn't want to wait a full year. In fact, Maribel would have been happy with three months, but wanted to allow time for people to prepare.

After a few more words from Jonas, Maribel took a new spot in a seat in the open. Jonas and the clergyman spoke a little longer and officially closed the ceremony. The public was invited to the coronation ball later that evening.

Maribel rose with the audience as Jonas turned and walked out. Part of her dreaded the next portion of the day. Many in the audience shuffled out of the church to return to their daily responsibilities, but tons of people lined up to meet her. She'd chosen comfortable shoes, but she might end up standing here for hours.

With the royal guard ensuring everything was safe and controlled, they first allowed Maribel's family and special guests to come see her. She got the tightest hugs, and Jonas soon made an appearance next to her, sliding his hand around her waist after exchanging handshakes and accepting congratulations.

Next, other members of the royal family got a chance to officially congratulate him and the couple, and then government officials and dignitaries from neighboring kingdoms. Last, tons of commoners who had patiently waited were given the chance to congratulate their new king and future queen.

After three hours, the couple finally pulled themselves away, seeking quiet to rest between the coronation and the ball that evening. After a short carriage ride to the castle, they made their way to a private sitting room where a buffet had been set up for them.

Jonas kicked off his shoes, shrugged off his decorated jacket, and undid a couple of buttons on his shirt. A servant had already taken his crown to protect and polish. Maribel kicked off her shoes as well, and they both guzzled water and loaded plates with food.

"That was a lot of talking," she said, her throat a little sore.

"It's part of what we do," he replied. "You'll get used to it."

Easing himself down onto a settee, he rested his plate on a side table. He extended his arms, and she smiled as she settled onto his lap and ate a grape. Wesley lay on the floor next to them.

"You did amazing, darling." He kissed her temple.

"You too. Your people are very lucky to have you." She scratched behind Wesley's ears.

"Our people? To have us?"

The words carried truth and familiarity. "Yes."

They cuddled and relaxed while filling their stomachs, chatting about how the event had gone, discussing how the ball would go.

He rubbed her knee as she finished her plate. "You don't have to say yes…" He hesitated.

"What?"

"Never mind." He shook his head.

"No…" She poked his arm. "Out with it."

"I…" He swallowed, averting his gaze. "We're still planning on not sharing a bed until the wedding, right?"

Her heart fluttered. They had agreed upon that. She was tempted to change those plans, but with the wedding only six months away, and them still getting to know each other, she wanted to take things slower. "I think I want to stick to that plan."

"Right. But … how would you feel if I … dream-walked with you sometimes before that? You in your bed, me in mine?"

She ran a finger along his arm. She wouldn't share his magic until their wedding, and even then, he had to train her how to use it. He had great power, and respected the harm and good he could do with it. To walk into anyone's dreams without an invitation would be terribly invasive.

Her cheeks warmed courtesy of a previous conversation regarding his magic and how it worked, what they'd be capable of doing together. He'd shyly admitted he didn't know what it would be like to make love in a shared dream once they both held the dreamer magic. She looked forward to finding out. But for now, how did she feel about him popping into her dreams at will?

Maribel snuck a kiss, his lips following hers as she pulled back. "Come say hi now and then. I trust you."

For another two hours, they cuddled and kissed, resting their feet and voices. Before she left to visit her special guests and freshen up before the ball, they practiced a couple of dances again. Jonas's royal upbringing made him the perfect dance partner, his kindness the perfect teacher.

***

This time, they would be introduced and enter together. His Majesty the King, and Lady Maribel.

The ballroom was lively with the music of a grandiose band, excited chatter competing in volume.

A gong sounded, and the room went silent as the couple stood at opposite ends of the entry to the top of the grand stairs. They were formally announced, then walked out, meeting in the middle.

They had both changed their clothes. She wore a deep blue dress this time, accented with ribbon—a fancy new white silk ribbon layered with her favorite old green one. He, as always, looked refined and devastatingly handsome. His cologne was just as enchanting. Maribel hooked her arm through his, and they descended the stairs together.

While this event was to celebrate the coronation, it felt more like a celebration for them, and in a way it was. It was also an engagement party, and they would fully be on display for all to see as a couple.

Jonas thanked the people for coming, and invited them all to indulge in the food and drinks, dance and conversation. No one moved, not until the first dance took place.

He turned to Maribel, bowing and offering his hand. Her cheeks ached from so much smiling. She'd never smiled so much in her life. She accepted by giving him her hand, and he pulled her close.

The band struck up a tune, and the world watched as the two of them glided across the floor. Maribel had taken dance lessons, as had everyone in her acquaintance, but she'd never mastered more complicated moves. She and Jonas had selected a few dances she felt comfortable enough to do, and she happily allowed him to lead.

In their relationship, in their life, in their roles, he may always be a little ahead of her. He had to teach her politics, and strategy, and magic. She would balance him in other ways, and he constantly reminded her that she was no less.

As the dance ended, he kissed her forehead. The band started a new song, and the rest of the room was invited to dance.

It would be a long night—more talking and dancing with friends, family, and dignitaries. Dignitaries didn't hesitate to snatch Maribel up, taking the opportunity to interview her on the dance floor. She held her own. When they asked questions she couldn't genuinely or officially weigh in on yet, she defaulted to the same answer, that Jonas would be the person to bring that up with. She knew when the topic was over her head. Her heart warmed, though, when they asked about her family. Jonas had promised to take good care of them, and she believed him. Her parents had already thanked him for his generosity, but they primarily wanted help in recovering her father's suffering business, and in expanding it. The fact that she could help even here and now brought her genuine pride, because she could direct important people to her father's business to help it grow. Not everyone had such an opportunity.

After hours at the ball, she was beyond exhausted. They both were. They stole a few smooches as he dropped her off at her chambers, but they quickly retired to their own beds. She'd been too exhausted to even bathe away the sweat and grime from the long day.

Her mattress was soft and supportive, her sleep deep. Sometime during the night, a light tap alerted her to Jonas's presence. She remained as she was, floating in the black emptiness of a dreamless sleep. *Jonas? You can come in.*

A dream bloomed around her, around them. They stood on a sandy beach, a light breeze wafting from the gentle waves on what she presumed was the southern sea.

"I missed you," he said, gliding his hands down her bare arms.

She smiled wide. "Didn't we just spend all day together?" She hugged him, and only then realized they weren't fully clothed, but he'd picked tasteful swimming clothes for them.

"I still missed you." His expression was soft, adoring. "Do you like this dream?"

She glanced around the private beach and dipped her toes in the water. A sunset lingered on the horizon, and the water was warm. "I love it." Since she had not been dreaming, he'd crafted something for them.

"What do you say to this location for our honeymoon?"

Her heart beat wildly as he slid his hands onto her back. "I'd be happy with you anywhere," she said. "But I think this is perfect." They exchanged a smile.

Time could warp in dreams, so they were probably only there for an hour, but it felt like an entire day. They swam, and built sandcastles, and kissed, and chatted like old friends. It may only be a dream, but it was a slice of heaven.

It was also a promise they shared. Ruling a kingdom would be tiresome and stressful at times. They may not always have the chance to take time together, at least not while awake. But they had an opportunity few did—no matter how busy their lives, they could always make time for each other in their dreams.

~Don't forget to leave a review!~

On Amazon, Goodreads, StoryGraph, and/or anywhere else this book can be found.

**Sign up for J. Houser's newsletter
For a free download of
*The Dreamer Prince!***

JHouserWrites.com

Also, connect with the author here:
On YouTube, TikTok, Facebook, Instagram, and Twitter under:
JHouserWrites

Other books by J. Houser

Also in the *Magic in the Match* fairy tale romance series:

The Hatanii Bride is another standalone novelette, inspired by a Polish fairy tale and set in a Polynesian atmosphere. It has all the best tropes—arranged marriage, enemies-to-lovers, and more!

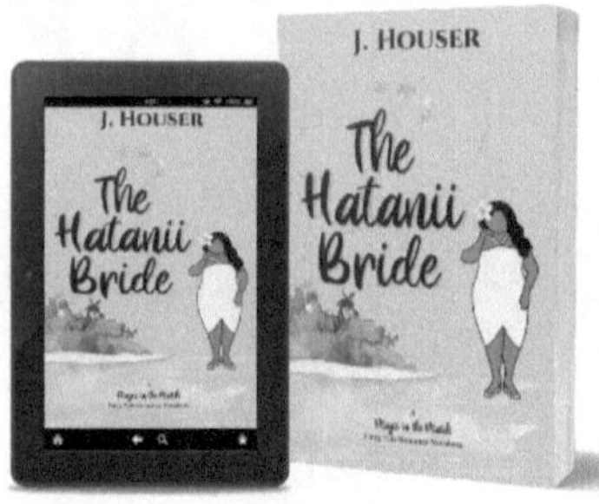

THE SEEDER WARS TRILOGY

THE HEIR'S DUOLOGY

Seeder Wars is a Young Adult Contemporary Romantic Fantasy series featuring unique magic, botanical beings, spies, & assassins. The series starts with a central trilogy and expands to a spin-off duology (& more on the way!)

The Green Lands Fantasy Coloring Book allows you to enjoy the magic & nature of the Green Lands realm, as featured in the *Seeder Wars* series!

(No knowledge of the series is necessary to enjoy the coloring book.)

Looking for an elegant and fun way to keep track of your reads?

Check out this series of premium book journals, easily disguised as regular novels on your shelf! Each includes entry pages for 250 books, as well as places to list your TBR, DNFs, and more!

Looking for more midsize and plus-size fairy tale retellings? An abridged version of *The Dream Trials* is included in the *Femme Fairytales* anthology along with several more retellings by other authors.

Stickers

Signed Bookplates

Book merch & more
on JHouserWrites.com/shop

Bookmarks